# I Met a Dinosaur

Text copyright © 1997 by Jan Wahl    Illustrations copyright © 1997 by Chris Sheban    Designed by Rita Marshall
Previously published in 1997. This edition published in 2015 by Creative Editions.    P.O. Box 227. Mankato. MN 56002 USA
Creative Editions is an imprint of The Creative Company    www.thecreativecompany.us
Printed in China    **Library of Congress Cataloging-in-Publication Data** Wahl. Jan. I met a dinosaur / by Jan Wahl; illustrated by Chris Sheban.
Summary: After a visit to a museum of natural history, a young girl begins to see dinosaurs everywhere.    ISBN 978-1-56846-233-2
1. Stories in rhyme. 2. Dinosaurs—Fiction. 3. Imagination—Fiction. I. Sheban. Chris. illustrator. II. Title.
PZ8.3.W133Iae 2015    [E]—dc22    2014022590
First edition 9 8 7 6 5 4 3 2 1

# I Met a Dinosaur

by Jan Wahl

illustrated by Chris Sheban

Creative Editions

I
met a
dinosaur
and a
dinosaur
met me
at the Museum
of Natural
History.

Triceratops

"**G**irl, it's just bones, gray bones," they say. This wasn't true for me when we left that day.

Allosaurus

On
Monday night
riding home in the dark,
an apatosaurus crossed
the road near the park.

Ma was driving.
Pa shook his head.
"That's only a moose,
nothing more,"
he said.

Apatosaurus

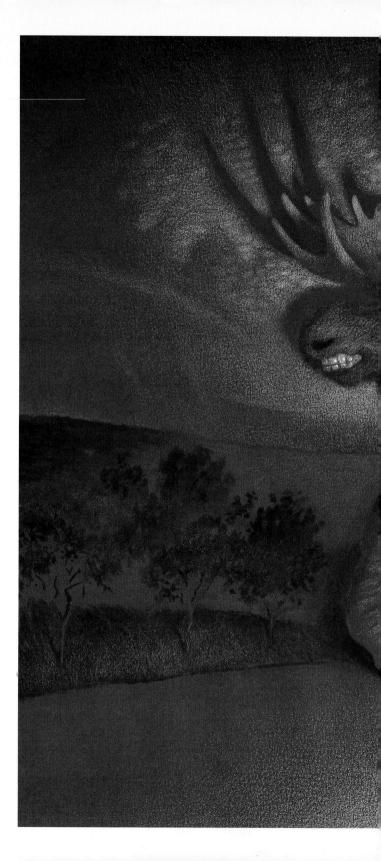

**N**ear
our house,
about a block away,
on Tuesday I saw
a stegosaurus at play.

She was at the gas station
amid pumps, cars, and more,
rolling her eyes
by the station's front door.

Stegosaurus

Late on Wednesday
out behind our shed,
I heard a rattle
and a bang,
something looking
to be fed.

"A tiny dimetrodon,"
I sang as I stared
through the glass.
"Just a raccoon,"
called Pa.
"Or a cow
eating grass."

Dimetrodon

**A**t

the edge of town

near the railroad track

stand two electric towers,

lights shining in the black.

On Thursday

I saw a blink from the towers.

Hello, triceratops.

I stood there for hours.

Triceratops

On
Friday Pa and I
rowed far out on the lake.
It started to rain.
I saw something give a shake.

Pa let out a sigh,
"A log that something's
sitting on."
"No, no!" I cried.
"It looks like an iguanodon."

Iguanodon

**S**aturday morning
when all was still,
I took my wagon to roll
down Tip Top Hill.

Looking down
from the height,
I got a push from
the breeze.
That was no moving van
by the buttonwood trees.

A
tyrannosaurus
peered past
a leafy limb.
With his short
arm, he waved.
I waved
back at
him.

Tyrannosaurus rex

# Sunday

afternoon was perfect
to fly my kite.
High up it flew!
The string pulled tight.

I squinted my eye.
I could see it just fine.
A pterodactyl pulled
on the end of the line.

Pterodactyl

I
rushed home to tell.
"Fine, girl, fine. Have a drink."
Mom handed me a glass
of water from the sink.

Now up to bed
we went all three,
Ma, Pa,
and also me.

"Lights off!
Stop reading.
It's time for bed.
Close your eyes, girl,
lay down your head."

I stayed quite still,
I turned my thoughts down.
Outside the window, a fog
crept round the town.

Diplodocus

Before
I sleep,
I can't count
sheep.

I see dinosaurs
everywhere.
Could be one
sitting in my
chair.

Dinosaurs

# Dinosaurs and Other Creatures

(In Order of Appearance)

**TRICERATOPS.** "three-horned face," had a huge head, seven feet long. It had one stubby horn on its nose and two horns above its eyes. Weighing six to twelve tons, it survived on the plants of the forest. It was one of the last dinosaurs on Earth.

**ALLOSAURUS.** "different lizard," was one of the largest dinosaurs in North America—forty feet long from head to tail. On its hind legs, it stood fifteen feet tall. It was a meat-eater and a very powerful animal with strong leg muscles and sharp claws on its front feet.

**APATOSAURUS.** "deceptive lizard," lived near rivers, browsing on treetops and ferns. A solid animal with an extremely long neck and an even longer tail, it measured seventy to eighty feet. It weighed about thirty tons, the equivalent of five elephants. Some specimens of Apatosaurus were named "Brontosaurus," or "thunder lizard."

**STEGOSAURUS.** "roof lizard," had a small head, a back ridged with plates, and a spiky tail. About the length of a bus, it grazed on ferns and shrubs and could defend itself by swinging its dangerous tail.

**DIMETRODON.** "two measures of teeth," was a four-legged, meat-eating reptile that lived before the dinosaurs. Besides having two different kinds of teeth (actually, it had three), it's known for the webbed sail on its back. The sail could have been used to attract mates, or it perhaps helped Dimetrodon control its body temperature. By turning the sail to catch the sun's rays, it could warm up.

**IGUANODON.** "iguana tooth," walked on its back feet, using its front feet to pull down leaves to eat. It might have defended itself by sticking its spiky thumb into its enemy. This four-ton dinosaur, thirty-three feet long, traveled in herds.

**TYRANNOSAURUS.** "tyrant lizard," one of the largest meat-eating dinosaurs, ran on its two hind legs. From nose to tail, it was forty feet long and had fifty to sixty teeth of different sizes and shapes. Unlike many dinosaurs, it had eyes that faced forward, allowing it to judge distances.

**PTERODACTYLS.** "wing fingers," were a group of flying reptiles with wingspans ranging from that of a sparrow to that of a small airplane. They ate fish and other sea creatures and used the wind to soar with their featherless wings.

**DROMICEIOMIMUS.** "emu mimic," was as big as an ostrich or emu and looked like one, too. It lived in the forests of western Canada and preyed on small animals. It could run more than fifty miles per hour.

**DIPLODOCUS.** "double beam," was one of the longest dinosaurs, measuring ninety feet from head to tail. It had a barrel-shaped body, stubby legs, a long neck and whiplike tail, and a tiny head.